John T. King

Greenmount.

John T. King

Greenmount.

ISBN/EAN: 9783337288983

Printed in Europe, USA, Canada, Australia, Japan

Cover: Foto ©Andreas Hilbeck / pixelio.de

More available books at **www.hansebooks.com**

"Behold the place where they laid Him."

Greenmount.

"They shall bring him unto the grave, and he shall be laid in the tomb, and the clods of the valley shall be sweet unto him."

"Oh, that Thou wouldest hide me in the grave, that Thou wouldest keep me secret until Thy wrath be past."

J. T. King, M. D.

Greenmount.

Greenmount.

IS there a soul so callous as not to be touched and awed upon entering this sacred and lovely City of the Dead? In all directions broad, umbrageous avenues and sequestered paths extend and ramify—all pervaded by a solemn, holy tenebrosity, produced by the dense, folial canopy and interlacing boughs of Greenmount's majestic forest trees

> "The groves were God's first temples,
> 'Ere man learned to hew the shaft
> or lay the architrave."

In these arborial temples, amid deep silence, humbly knelt the Christian patriarch of old, and poured forth his supplication to the most high God.

Almighty Father, Thy hand hath reared these venerable oaks; Thou didst weave this leafy canopy; Thou didst look down upon the barren earth, and at Thy command forthwith arose in all their grandeur these venerable trees, and all this sylvan beauty.

Here they stand solemn and silent, fit shrine for the humble worshipper to kneel beside, to hold communion with his Lord and Maker.

This mighty oak, at whose feet I stand, beside which I am dwarfed almost to insignificance, in his green coronal of leaves made by the Almighty's hand, in majesty far excels the mightiest monarchs of the proud world beyond.

Beneath this cool and verdant dome, in these hallowed shades, incline Thou my heart to fervent prayer and holy meditation — impress me with the wisdom, beauty, sublimity and order of Thy works.

All around the heavenly stillness is unbroken, save by the gentle footfall of the sorrowing visitor or mournful pilgrim, tearfully wending his or her way to the spot

"where they laid him."

In joyous springtime, at nature's resurrection, and in genial summer, is heard the joyous warblings of

Delighted birds

as they disport amid the boughs and foliage of the leafy grove, enlivened by vitalizing sun-beams and vernal air, supremely happy in their sacred sylvan home.

Ever and anon is heard the metallic tinklings and liquid murmur of yon crystal spring that from the rocky cleft or mossy nook wells forth to lave refreshingly and quench the thirst—to minister alike to the humblest flower, the tiniest grass-spear and the majestic tree.

Amid these solemn shades, in this silent City of the Dead, in this monumental wilderness, all can realize that this world is but vanity, and ask themselves the question " What will it profit one to gain the whole world and lose his soul."

Here the arrogant and proud can linger, and be convinced that they are but the dust of the earth, and that " the paths of glory lead but to the grave."

In Greenmount's sacred avenues and quiet walks the Christian will delight to roam, comforted by the assurance that the dark and silent grave is but the portal of eternal bliss, and that they will surely hear at the final day the joyful salutation, " well done, thou good and faithful servant, enter thou into the joy of thy Lord."

One may see, perchance, the tottering, hoary pilgrim, bowed upon his staff, and with up-turned eyes, imploring,

" Lord, let not my gray hairs go down into the grave, until I have told the rising generation of thy mercy and loving kindness."

Amid this floral bloom and garniture could little children delight to roam, knowing from parental teaching that they are especially dear unto, and constantly in their Heavenly Father's care and keeping, and that he has enjoined to,

" Suffer little children to come unto him, and to forbid them not,—for of such is the kingdom of Heaven."

Here the inquisitive, tender mind would be prone to ask,

"Mother, O where is that radiant shore
Where we shall meet to part no more,
Is it where flowers of the orange blows
Where the warm bright sun forever glows?"
　　"Not there, not there, my child."

"Is it where the feathery palm trees rise
And the date grows ripe under sunny skies
Is it far away in some region old
Where the rivers wander o'er sands of gold,
And the pearl gleams forth from the coral strand,
Is it there, sweet mother, that happy land?"
　　"Not there, not there, my child."

"Eye hath not seen it, my gentle boy;
Ear hath not heard its deep sounds of joy;
Dreams cannot picture a world so fair,
'Tis beyond the bright clouds.—it is there.
　　My child."

" To all ages and conditions is such a hallowed spot inviting and comforting, here can be enjoyed moments of respite from sin and folly, and calm intervals for profitable reflection and self-examination."

On every hand are ornate monuments and graceful shafts and tablets, chaste in design, and wrought in the sculptor's highest art; upon almost every monument and grassy mound are floral garlands of exquisite flowers and lovely "immortelles," glittering and fragrant with the morning dew; daily beside them may be seen lingering and kneeling the weeping mourner—perchance some sorrowing mother, with up-turned eyes, and hands clasped convulsively in prayer, lamenting in deep bitterness of woe and refusing to be comforted. Here can be heard the orphan's plaint and the widow's wail and the father's manly lamentation, as in convulsive utterances he exclaims as did King David:

"Alas my noble boy, that thou shouldst die,
Thou who wert made so beautifully fair,
That death should settle in thy glorious eye
And leave his cold chill in thy clustering hair."
How could he mark thee for the silent tomb.

And the disconsolate partner in life, of the one that sleeps in death, in frantic anguish finds utterance in sad soliloquy,

"The grave hath won thee:
Must thy dark tresses to the cold earth be flung,
Will thou no more with thy sweet smile
——Come to greet me?"

——"Farewell,
'Tis hard to give thee up,
With death so like a gentle slumber on thee,
Like a bruised reed, I am waiting—waiting—
For God to call me like a wanderer home."

The wordling can solace himself with that sweetest elegy,

Beneath these rugged oaks, that elm tree's shade,
  Where heaves the turf in many a mouldering heap,
Each in his narrow cell forever laid,
  The rude forefathers of the hamlet sleep.

Can storied urn or animated bust,
  Back to its mansion call the fleeting breath,
Can honor's voice provoke the silent dust
  Or flattery soothe the dull, cold ear of death.

The boast of heraldry, the pomp of power,
  And all that beauty, all that earth ere gave,
Await alike the inevitable hour,
  The paths of glory lead but to the grave.

One morn I missed him on the accustomed hill
  Along the heath, and near his favorite tree,
Another came—nor yet beside the rill,
  Nor up the lawn, nor at the wood was he.

The next, with dirges due, and sad array,
  Slow through the churchway path me saw him borne
Approach and read, for thou can'st read the lay,

Graved on the stone beneath yon aged thorn.

No further seek his merits to disclose
Or draw his frailties from their dread abode,
There they alike in trembling hope repose,
The bosom of his father and his God.

CHAPEL IN GREENMOUNT.

IN front of the main entrance to Greenmount, upon a verdant, gracefully rounded eminence, stands the chapel, a
Gothic structure, of brown-stone. It is elaborately and ornately sculptured, presenting a strikingly beautiful specimen
of ecclesiastical architecture.

The design is from one of the chapels in Westminster Ab-
bey, London.

GREENMOUNT'S

MONUMENTS AND TOMBS

OF THE

GOOD, BRAVE AND BEAUTIFUL.

A GRAVE wherever found, preaches a short and pithy lesson to the soul ; and it is well for us occasionally to pass
an hour in the silence of God's acre, as a species of soul's
exercise or mental lesson, to remind us of the great aims and
objects of a true man's life, and we cannot do better than
quote the beautiful reflections of Washington Irving :

" Oh, the grave!—the grave ! it buries every error—covers every
defect—extinguishes every resentment! From its peaceful bosom
spring none but fond regrets and tender recollections. Who can
look down upon the grave even of an enemy, and not feel a com-
punctious throb that he should ever have warred with the poor
handful of earth that lies mouldering before him ?

But the grave of those we loved—what a place for meditation!
There it is that we call up a long review the whole history of virtue and gentleness, and the thousand endearments lavished upon
us. almost unheeded in the daily intercourse of intimacy—there it
is tdat we dwell upon the tenderness, the solemn, awful tenderness of the parting scene. The bed of death, with all its stifled

griefs—its noiseless attendance—its mute, watchful assiduities. The last testimonies of expiring love! The feeble, fluttering thrilling!—pressure of the hand. The last fond look of the glazing eye turning upon us even from the threshold of existence! The faint, faltering accents, struggling in death to give one more assurance of affection?

Ay, go to the grave of buried love, and meditate! There settle the account with thy conscience for every past benefit unrequited—every past endearment unregarded, of that departed being, who can never—never—never return to be soothed by thy contrition!

If thou art a child, and hast ever added a sorrow to the soul or a furrow to the silvered brow of an affectionate parent—if thou art a husband, and hast ever caused the fond bosom that ventured its whole happiness in thy arms to doubt one moment of thy kindness or thy truth—if thou art'a friend, and hast ever wronged, in thought or word or deed, the spirit that generously confided in thee—if thou art a lover, and hast ever given one unmerited pang to that true heart which now lies cold and still beneath thy feet: —then be sure that every unkind look, every ungracious word every ungentle action, will come thronging back upon thy memory, and knocking dolefully at thy soul—then be sure that thou wilt lie down sorrowing and repentant on the grave, and utter the unheard groan and pour the unavailing tear: more deep, more bitter, because unheard and unavailing.

Then weave thy chaplet of flowers, and strew the beauties of nature about the grave; console thy broken spirit, if thou canst with these tender, yet futile tributes of regret; but take warning by the bitterness of this thy contrite affliction over the dead, and henceforth be more faithful and affectionate in the discharge of thy duties to the living "

THE first interment that occurred in Greenmount was that of an infant, December 29, 1839, which was memorialized by a beautiful poem from the gifted pen of S. TEACKLE WALLIS, Esq., of the Baltimore bar.

GRAVE OF MAJOR SAMUEL RINGGOLD

Once inclosed by a fence of Mexican gun-barrels and bayonets captured in the Mexican war, now a plain marble slab, bears the inscription, " Mortally wounded at Palo Alto, May 8, 1845, died at Corpus Christi, May 10, 1846." By his side sleeps the gallant brother, CADWALLADER RINGGOLD, Rear-Admiral, U. S. Navy.

GRAVE OF COL. WILLIAM H. WATSON,

Commander of the Baltimore Batallion in the Mexican war; was killed at Monterey.

GRAVE OF A SOLDIER AND DEFENDER OF 1812 AND 1814,

GEN. WM. H. WINDER.

A tall obelisk with urn, and a medallion portrait of deceased. Gen. Winder, of the Confederate Army, was a son of this hero of 1812.

GRAVE OF THE FOUNDER OF ODD-FELLOWSHIP IN AMERICA.

PAST GRAND SIRE THOMAS WILDEY.

Thomas Wildey was born in England in 1783. Died in 1861. Together with two others he established on the 26th day of April, 1819, Washington Lodge, No. 1, in the city of Baltimore. A beautiful marble monument is erected to his memory in the centre of Broadway, north of Baltimore Street, upon a commanding eminence.

MONUMENT OF THE GREAT TRAGEDIAN BOOTH,

And his children, among the latter are the remains of

JOHN WILKES BOOTH.

JOHN WILKES BOOTH as is universally known, assassinated President Lincoln at the Opera House in Washington, fled to Virginia, was then captured and shot in self-defence, in an old tobacco barn. His remains were clandestinely buried by the U. S. Government, and for a long time the Government refused to betray the spot, or surrender his remains to his friends.

MONUMENT IN LOT OF ENOCH PRATT.

Scotch granite, which is handsomely variegated, stone capable of the finest polish.

MONUMENT OF
JAMES O. LAW, Ex-Mayor of Baltimore.

Mayor O. Law died June 6th, 1847, of ship fever, in the service of the destitute.

MONUMENT TO ANOTHER MARTYR, FERGUSON.

When the yellow fever raged with such fearful fury in the city of Norfolk, Ferguson, a Baltimorean, at the head of the citizens, toiled day and night, relieving the sick and burying the dead, and at last was stricken down by the merciless pestilence.

MARBLE MONUMENT OF WILLIAM M'DONALD,
Ornate and Costly

MONUMENT OF ROBERT OLIVER,
Proprietor of Greenmount.

Here lies the remains of the former owner of this beautiful spot, where as his country seat he spent so many happy hours of his life. A tall Gothic, ornately sculptured shaft tells the story of the instability of all earthly things, and teaches with sublime impressiveness that every path of life however illustrious or obscure leads but to the grave.

GRAVE OF WILLIAM SCHLEY.

A scholar and eminent lawyer of the Baltimore Bar.

LOT OF BENJAMIN F. CATOR.

An exquisite statue of an Angel teaching immortality from the Book of Life.

LOT OF HON. THOMAS SWANN, U. S. SENATOR.

A massive cross of pure white marble, and an elegant marble tablet at its side. Here beneath the roses that exhale their fragrance and bright flowers rest in the embrace of death the beautiful and good in life.

LOT OF HUGH SISSON.

Two marble sleeping infants, executed in the sculptor's highest art, in commemoration of deceased children.

GRAVE OF WILLIAM WARREN,

A CELEBRATED ACTOR.

MONUMENT OF WILLIAM T. WALTERS.

This is one of the most expensive, and beautifully designed monuments in Greenmount. It was erected by Mr. William T. Walters, of Baltimore, over the remains of his wife. It represents a female strewing flowers on the grave beneath. It is of bronze and was designed by Rhinehart, the Baltimore sculptor.

MONUMENT OF CAPTAIN GEORGE RUSSELL,

SHAFT AND ANCHOR.

MONUMENT OF JOHN BOYD,

TENNESSEE MARBLE.

MONUMENT OF JOSEPH BOURY.

MONUMENT OF R. A. TAYLOR.

MONUMENT OF JOHN G. McDONOGH,

Founder of the McDonogh School for Boys, near Baltimore.

Born in the city of Baltimore in 1779. Died in New Orleans, 1850. The mount consists of a heavy granite base, supporting a marble pedestal 14 feet in height, upon which rests the statue of the deceased, larger than life size. The pedestal contains an inscription by himself, and the rules that he has observed for his guidance in life.

———

GRAVE OF AN EXPLORER,

COMMODORE WM. F. LYNCH, U. S. NAVY.

Upon this tablet is a sword and anchor; Commodore Lynch commanded the U. S. Exploring Expedition of 1848 to the Dead Sea and River Jordan.

"META."

White marble sarcophagus, covered with heavy marble pall, one of the most elaborately executed, and beautiful in design in Greenmount.

GRAVE OF JOHNS HOPKINS,

The Millionaire and Founder of the Johns Hopkins Hospital and University.

LOT AND MONUMENT OF
ANDREW M'LAUGHLIN AND DAVID BARNUM.

In this lot are two tombs, upon one is a marble sleeping infant.

MONUMENT OF "TO OUR SISTER,"
ELIZABETH ANNE McPHAIL.

Marble angel.

MONUMENT OF SAMUEL WILHELM.

Ornamented with exquisitely wrought marble drapery, vines and anchor. In the same lot, a life-sized figure of a female leaning upon an anchor.

MONUMENT OF HENRY KNELL,

"To our Mother," MARY ANN KNELL.

Of Italian marble, ornamented with flowers, vines and drapery.

LOT OF THOMAS WINANS.

Inclosed by granite railing, massive flat vault, covered with heavy Tennessee marble slab.

MONUMENT OF ASHUR CLARKE.

Tomb and cross, erected by his former pupils.

MONUMENT OF GOODWIN C. WILLIAMS.

Tall Ionic shaft, with floral capital.

MONUMENT OF
WILLIAM BOND, TO WIFE ELIZABETH.
Full-sized female.

LOT AND MONUMENT OF JOHN WICKS AND HERMAN WOODS.

MONUMENT OF
ANN ELIZA, WIFE OF WM. H. CUNNINGHAM.
Angel with trumpet.

MONUMENT AND BEAUTIFUL CROWN OF
LOUISA E., WIFE OF GEORGE W. RHEA,
And daughter of Capt. Wingate. Died Feb. 4, 1873, in the 26th year of her age.

" Blest was her latest hour,
She died forgiving and forgiven,
Earth was no place for her to dwell,
Her resting place is Heaven."

MONUMENT OF RICHARD MASON,
Female Figure.

MONUMENT OF JOHN CONTEE,
Shaft and Urn.

TOMB OF ALBERT SCHUMACHER,
High massive granite base, surmounted by tomb.

MONUMENT OF NOAH WALKER.
White marble shaft, female with child in arms in niche, lot surrounded by massive stone railing.

MONUMENT OF J. COLTON.
Female figure and cross.

LOT OF REVERDY JOHNSON.
Grave, with large marble cross.

LOT OF ROBERT GARRETT AND HENRY GARRETT.
Shaft and tomb.

MONUMENT OF GEORGE BROWN.
Marble shaft.

MONUMENT OF CAVANAGH.
Marble figure and cross.

MONUMENT OF JOHN COATES.

MONUMENT OF HUGH GELSTON
Surmounted by an elaborate urn.

MONUMENT OF ZENUS BARNUM.

MONUMENT OF H. J. ROBERTS.
Female seated in a rocking chair.

MONUMENT OF THOMAS.

Marble base, representing a pile of rocks upon which rests a shaft, surmounted by an urn, embellished with vines spirally winding the shaft.

MONUMENT OF SAMUEL CAUGHEY.
Weeping female and urn.

MONUMENT OF
ANNIE E., WIFE OF VIRGINIUS GADDESS.
Marble angel, pointing heavenward.

MONUMENT OF GEHRMANN.

Shaft and female leaning on an anchor, exquisite in design and execution.

MONUMENT OF GREENWAY.

Figure reading from a book, with a dog fondling beside.

MONUMENT OF JACOB HORN.

Female figure

MONUMENT OF A. S. ABELL, TO WIFE.

PUBLIC MAUSOLEUM.

The public mausoleum of Greenmount is of granite and of the Egyptian order of sepulchral architecture.

PRIVATE MAUSOLEA AND VAULTS.

VAULT OF GEARY AND WEALE.

This is a magnificent vault, it contains a finely sculptured figure of St. Joseph.

VAULT OF D. L. HAMMERSLEY.

VAULT OF THE WEST AND DRYDEN FAMILY.

This is one of the handsomest in Greenmount.

VAULT OF JAMES STIRRATT.

The doors of this vault are nearly all the time open, and in the vestibule may be seen beautiful statues and fresh flowers, over the portal is inscribed in golden letters, *memento mori*.

VAULT OF JOHN H. WEAVER, UNDERTAKER.

This is a spacious and elegant vault, decorated with art and good taste, it contains about eighty bodies, among them is that of a child which has been there seventeen years and is now in a good state of preservation.

VAULT OF HENRY PLACIDE.
Marble figure and anchor.

BOYCE VAULT.

VAULT OF JAMES BATES.

VAULT OF PHILLIP CHAPPELL.

DEDICATION

— OF —

GREENMOUNT CEMETERY.

GREENMOUNT was the name given to the country seat of the late ROBERT OLIVER, in the vicinity of Baltimore. During his life, Mr. Oliver spared no expense in beautifying it; and aided by its natural advantages, he left it, at his death, a highly ornamented and most lovely spot. It was purchased from his heirs by an association of gentlemen, who appropriated sixty acres of it to the establishment of the public Cemetery, whose dedication gave rise to the ceremonial, of which the following pages are the record.

The dedication took place on the grounds, in the open air, in a grove of forest trees, on the evening of Saturday, July 13th, 1839.

The hour for commencing the ceremonies of the dedication having arrived, the Musical Association of Baltimore, who lent their most valuable services on the occasion, sang the following chorale, from the Oratorio of St. Paul:

"Sleepers wake, a voice is calling,
It is the watchman on the walls:
Thou city of Jerusalem!
For lo! the bridegroom comes!
Arise, and take your lamps!
Hallelujah!
Awake, his kingdom is at hand,
Go forth to meet your Lord!"

PRAYER,

BY REV. WILLIAM E. WYATT, RECTOR OF SAINT PAUL'S.

OUR Father in heaven, we who dwell in houses of clay, and are crushed before the moth, approach to render homage to Him that inhabiteth eternity. Strangers and pilgrims as we are upon the earth, we would lay the foundations of a city of the dead   And taught by this narrow field, destined to be the receptacle of successive generations, we discern the vanity and frailty of our nature, and we take refuge at the foot of thy throne, O Most Mighty, Creator of the ends of the earth, whose judgments are a great deep.   Before the mountains were brought forth, or ever the earth and the worlds were made from everlasting to everlasting, thou, and thou only, art GOD. Together with the adoring tribute of creatures to their Creator, we offer thee our thanksgivings, for all the dispensations of thy love and bounty, thy care and providence, thy forbearance and pity. More especially we praise thee for the glorious hope of immortality; and that beyond our bed of corruption, and our sleep in dust, there is a bright world of perfections and privileges, spiritual and like thyself, everlasting. Great God, we thank thee for all the means and instruments of attaining this unspeakable gift; for thy written word, with its mighty attestations; for thy life-giving doctrines; thy strengthening ordinance; thy consoling graces. Above all, we thank thee for sending eternal redemption to us by the blood of thine own incarnate Son. O accept our worship and praise, that thou art reconciling the world unto thyself by Jesus Christ, not imputing their trespasses unto them; and that in him we have "complete redemption."

It is thy gracious promise, Lord, who dost guide thy people in thy strength to thy holy habitation, that if we lean not to our own understanding, but commit our way unto the Lord, thou wilt bring it to pass. We therefore come before thee to invoke thy blessing upon the undertaking of thy servants here assembled, who, according to the example of the patriarchs and thy people of old, are about to set apart " a field for a burying place," when we, and ours, shall be gathered unto our fathers. The earth is thine, O Lord, and the fullness thereof, and meet it is that we should solemnly dedicate to the blended purposes of religion and charity, a portion of what thou hast given to our use. Meet it is that here, beneath the shade of the majestic wood, in a holy solitude and silence, they who have fulfilled their pilgrimage, and rest from their labors, should wait in peace the summons of the Resurrection morn. Our Father, take this sequestered asylum to thy special providence. Ever spread over it the shadow of thy wings. With gentler dispensation than of old, when sin had driven our fathers from Eden, let angels, though unseen, guard its entrance. Let not the foot of pride or folly, or violence, come near to unhallow it. And although no voice of admonition can reach the dull ear of death, nor prayer avail to change the doom which thou hast here sealed, yet gracious Lord, may each grassy mound, and each marble memorial, utter a thrilling warning to the living, and fill this page of man's history with lessons of wisdom to every heart.

When to any one among us, thy decree shall go forth, "dust thou art, and unto dust shalt thou return;" and when the mourning train has hither borne the loved one to the house appointed for all living, and with holy rites we seek at thy hands consolation and strength; have thou respect unto the prayer of thy ministering servants, and to their supplication, O Lord our God, to hearken to the cry of sorrow, and to the prayer of faith, which may reach thy footstool from these sepulchres; and hear thou in heaven, thy dwelling place, and when thou hearest, forgive.

God of consolation, may thy Spirit ever be present to minister to the bereaved whom thy providence shall draw within these sacred enclosures; and while resigned, they bow meekly before thy sovereign, though sometimes inscrutable, decrees, inspire, Lord, the soothing reflection, that, " to die is gain ; " that here the wicked cease from troubling, and the weary are at rest ; that here temptation expires, and each toilsome task is fulfilled, and transient sorrow turned into everlasting joy.   When in bitter anguish they shall look into the graves here to be opened as into a fearful abyss, dividing them from all that can render life joyous, O do thou teach them, that that separation shall be short; that quickly shall all the scenes and illusions of time vanish ; and that, in the land of spirits, soon shall every holy tie be again bound, and severed hearts be forever re-united.

All-wise God, in this vestibule of the unseen world, where through the clustering oaks, the perpetual dirge of winds seems the response of awful rites within, inspire us with lessons of heavenly-mindedness and devotion.   From yonder stately mansion,* where once was heard the viol and the harp, but henceforth the sanctuary of offices for the dead, let us learn the instability of earthly things. From the slow funeral pageant, which entering with touching ritual, within these walls, in the proud mausoleum shall deposit the remains of the professor of rank and wealth, may we all be taught the folly of pride. And when the learned and the mighty shall here say to corruption, " thou art my father, and to the worm, thou art my mother and sister," may the friendless and the poor be inspired with contentment under the brief humilia- tions of their lot; and may they lay it to heart, that every path of life, however illustrious or obscure, ends alike but in a silent, nar- row cell.

In the view of the mouldering masses of corruption which shall soon swell this verdant turf, grant, most just and holy God that the madness of profligacy and excess, may be mightily urged upon every conscience. Teach the youthful and the passioned, musing in these avenues of the charnel house, that the ways of guilty pleasure lead to premature ruin, and that the wages of sin is death.   Here, let those who, in sottish idolatry of the world, are putting off from day to day the work of conversion to God, discern the danger of procrastination. Teach them the appalling truth, that " there is but a step between us and death." And while the tombs of the young, and the vigorous, and the bold, who have not lived out half their days, disclose the brief memorial of frustrated plans, and presumptuous hopes, may they startle every conscience into greater diligence of preparation for the Master's coming.

Here, in this quiet retreat from the turmoil of the world, teach us, O our Father, the fruitlessness of discord, and the little- ness of ambition. Looking into the noiseless chambers of the

*The seat of the late Robert Oliver, Esq., to be converted into a chapel for the Cemetery.

tomb, where once angry partisans lie down together without strife, and rival heroes find a calm resting place by each other's side, may our hearts be touched with the vanity of the feuds which disturb the peace of the world. Seeing here the end of glory, and the emptiness of triumphs, may we shun the vain conflicts of life, and seek supremely those things which are spiritual and eternal

When the wan and the weary child of disease, stands trembling beside an open sepulchre, and the vision of its dreary solitudes and eternal desolations sends a chill and shuddering foreboding into his heart, do thou, Lord, with thy rod and thy staff, sustain and cheer him. In the midst of that gloom, insinuate gently the triumphant assurance, "I know that my Redeemer liveth, and that he shall stand at the latter day upon the earth; and though, after my skin, worms destroy this body, yet in my flesh shall I see God, whom I shall see for myself, and mine eyes shall behold, and not another "

When holy bonds, cemented under thy sanction, are riven, and alliances of kindred or friendship are here dissolved; when standing thus upon the shore of eternity, we gaze upon the stranded bark of the now distant voyager, Lord, send to our hearts the deep inquiry, "Have the vows and the offices of love which I once assumed, been faithfully discharged? Was aught left undone for his temporal good? Withholding the meet returns of grateful affection, have I embittered the days of him whose remains now lie insensate before me? Owed I more zeal to his safety in that unchangeable state, where the never-dying spirit now is, beyond the reach of my aid, my prayers, and my attachment?" And grant gracious Lord, that salutary reflections like these, controlling our plans, and tempers, and conversation, may diffuse the spirit of gentleness and charity through the intercourse of such as survive.

Thou Great First Cause, Fountain of every good, who, by thy gospel, hast brought life and immortality to light, here teach the hapless sceptic the power of faith. Constrain him to inquire, what would be the refuge of his trembling spirit, in consecrating the cemetery, and rearing the mausoleum, if its darkness and gloom were the last stage of our being; if the dissolving elements of the body reveal the utter ruin of our nature; and if here an iron destiny called us to abandon forever to the desolations of the grave, the infant in its loveliness, the tender wife, and the cherished friend Pitying God, whence then could the voice of comfort arise! O fill all our hearts with a transporting sense of the value of our heavenly inheritance. Disclose to us the gate of the grave as the portals of immortality. And having this hope, may it be our great aim to purify ourselves even as thou art pure; to crucify the world in our hearts; in spirituality and heavenly mindedness, to be conformed to the likeness of Christ; to live by faith in the Son of God; that we may die in hope, and go down to the chambers of the dead, rich in all the promises of the everlasting covenant. And O God, who dost now make darkness thy pavilion about thee, in that day, when the last trumpet shall sound through all the secret caves of the ocean, and deep recesses of the earth, and when the voice of the archangel shall call forth the slumbering generations of men from the silent abode of ages, may we rise to a glorious resurrection, justified by faith, may we mingle in that great assembly, which cannot be numbered for multitude, with bodies glorified, affections sublimed, faculties perfected, to see Thee face to face, and to expatiate in immortal youth.

Our great Mediator, incarnate for man, who didst vouchsafe that thy sacred body should repose in the tomb of Joseph, own and bless this our undertaking. In thy name, we now dedicate this field " to be a burying place ; " that, in the bonds of a common faith, they whose remains shall be here consigned to their parent earth, may together rest in safety and hope. May the hallowing influences of thy gospel ever abide, in peaceful sway throughout this awful sanctuary of the dead And, when thou shalt stand at the latter day upon the earth, and the mountains shall quake, and the hills shall melt, may the awakening inhabitants of this city of the dead, through thy merits and intercession, O blessed Lord Jesus, have a building of God, a house not made with hands eternal in the heavens

---

H Y M N,

BY J. H. B. LATROBE, ESQ., SUNG BY MUSICAL ASSOCIATION.

WE meet not now where pillar'd aisles,
  In long and dim perspective fade :
No dome, by human hands uprear'd,
  Gives to this spot its solemn shade
Our temple is the woody vale,
  Whose forest cools the heated hours ;
Our incense is the balmy gale,
  Whose perfume is the spoil of flowers.

Yet here, where now the living meet,
  The shrouded dead ere long will rest,
And grass now trod beneath our feet,
  Will mournful wave above our breast
Here birds will sing their notes of praise,
  When summer hours are bright and warm :
And winter's sweeping winds will raise,
  The sounding anthems of the storm.

Then now, while life's warm currents flow,
  While restless throbs the anxious heart.
Teach us, oh Lord, thy power to know,
  Thy grace, oh Lord our God, impart:
That when, beneath this verdant soil,
  Our dust to kindred dust is given;
Our souls, released from mortal coil,
  May find, with thee, their rest in Heaven.

ADDRESS,

BY HON JOHN P. KENNEDY.

My Friends—

We have been called together at this place to distinguish, by an appropriate ceremonial, the establishment of the Greenmount Cemetery. It is gratifying to perceive, in this large assemblage of the inhabitants of our city, a proof of the interest they take in the accomplishment of this design. To a few of our public-spirited citizens we are indebted for this laudable undertaking, and I feel happy in the opportunity to congratulate them upon the eminent success with which their labors are likely to be crowned.

It is a natural sentiment that leads man to the contemplation of his final resting place. In the arrangement of the world there is no lack of remembrancers to remind us of dissolution. This unsteady navigation of life, with its adverse winds, its sunken rocks and secret shoals, its dangers of the narrow strait and open sea, is full of warning of shipwreck, and, even in its most prosperous conditions, awakens the mind to the perception that we are making our destined haven with an undesired speed.

Childhood has its dream of destruction; youth has its shudder at the frequent funeral pageant that obtrudes upon his gambols; manhood courts acquaintance with danger as the familiar price of success, and old age learns to look upon death with a cheerful countenance and to hail him as a companion This theatre of life, is it not even more appropriately a theatre of death? What is our title to be amongst the living, but a title derived from mortality? That extinction which tracked the footsteps of those who went before us and overtook them, made room for us, and brought us to this inheritance of air and light:—they who are to follow us will thank Death for their return upon earth. He is the patron of posterity, and the great provider for the present generation. We subsist by his labor; we are fed by his hand; to him we owe all this fabric of human production, these arts of civilization, these beneficent and beautifying toils, these wonder-working handicrafts and head fancies, that have filled this world with the marvels of man's genius. From Death springs Necessity, and from Necessity all man's triumphs over nature. Look abroad and tell me what has brought forth this beautiful scheme of

art which we call the world; what has invented all this enginery
of society; what has appointed it for man to toil, and given these
multiform rewards to his labor; why, with the rising sun, goes he
forth cheerily to his vocation, and endures the heat and burden of
the day with such good heart.   It is because Death has taught him
to strive against Hunger and Want.   Without such strife, this
fair garden were but a horrid wilderness—this populous array of
Christian men but some scattered horde of starving cannibals.
Again look abroad, and tell me what is this universal motion of
the elements, this perpetual progress from seed-time to harvest,
these silent workings of creation, and unceasing engenderments of
new forms,—what is this whole plan, but a mass of life ever
springing from the compost of death,—sensible, breathing
essences, melting away like flakes of snow, millions in every
moment, and out of their destruction new living things forever
coming forth?   Look to our own race.   Even as the forest sinks
to the earth under the sweep of the storm, or by the woodman's
axe, or by the touch of Time, so our fellow men fall before
the pestilence, or by the sword, or in the decay of age.   The dead
a thousandfold outnumber those that live:

> All that tread
> The globe, are but a handful to the tribes
> That slumber in its bosom.

In the midst of these tokens, do we stand in need of lectures to
remind us that we are but for a season, and that very soon we are
to be without a shadow on this orb?   Child of the dust, answer!
Confess, as I know in your secret breathings you must, that in the
watches of the night, when wakefulness has beset your pillow, or
in the chance seclusion of the day, when toil has been suspended
nay, even in the very eager importunity of business, and often in
the wildest moment of revelry, this question of death and his conditions has come unbidden to the mind, and with a strange
familiarity of fellowship has urged its claim to be entertained
in your meditations   Thus death grows upon us, and becomes, at
last, a domestic comrade thought.

Kind is it in the order of Providence that we are, in this wise,
bade to make ourselves ready for that inevitable day when
our bodies shall sleep upon the lap of our mother earth.   Wise in
us is it, too, to bethink ourselves of this in time, not only that we
may learn to walk humbly in the presence of our Creator, but
even for that lesser care, the due disposal of that visible remainder
which is to moulder into dust after the spirit has returned to God
who gave it.   Though to the eye of cold philosophy there may be
nothing in that remainder worthy of a monument, and though, in
contrast with the heaven lighted hopes of a Christian, it may
seem to be but dross too base to merit his care, yet still there is an
acknowledged longing of the heart that when life's calenture
is over, and its stirring errand done, this apt and delicate machine

by which we have wrought our work, this serviceable body whereof our ingenuity has found something to be vain, shall lie down to its long rest in some place agreeable to our living fancies, and be permitted, in undisturbed quiet, to commingle with its parent earth. The sentiment is strong in my bosom,—I doubt not it is shared by many,—to feel a keen interest in the mode and circumstances of that long sleep which it is appointed to each and all of us to sleep I do not wish to lie down in the crowded city. I would not be jostled in my narrow house,—much less have my dust give place to the intrusion of later comers : I would not have the stone memorial that marks my resting-place to be gazed upon by the business-perplexed crowd in their every day pursuit of gain, and where they ply their tricks of custom. Amidst this din and traffic of the living is no fit place for the dead. My affection is for the country, that God-made country, where Nature is the pure first-born of the Divinity, and all tokens around are of Truth. My tomb should be beneath the bowery trees, on some pleasant hill-side, within sound of the clear prattling brook ; where the air comes fresh and filled with the perfume of flowers; where the early violet greets the spring, and the sweet-briar blooms, and the woodbine ladens with the dews its fragrance ;

> Where the shower and the singing bird
> 'Midst the green leaves are heard—

where the yellow leaf of autumn shall play in the wind; and where the winter's snow shall fall in noiseless flakes and lie in unspotted brightness ;—the changing seasons thus symboling forth, even within the small precincts of my rest, that birth and growth and fall which marked my mortal state, and, in the renovation of Spring, giving a glad type of that resurrection which shall no less surely be mine.

I think it may be set down somewhat to the reproach of our country that we too much neglect this care of the dead. It betokens an amiable, venerating, and religious people, to see the tombs of their forefathers not only carefully preserved, but embellished with those natural accessories which display a thoughtful and appropriate reverence. The pomp of an overlabored and costly tomb scarcely may escape the criticism of a just taste: that tax which ostentation is wont to pay to the living in the luxury of sculptured marble dedicated to the dead, often attracts disgust by its extravagant disproportion to the merits of its object ; but a becoming respect for those from whom we have sprung, an affectionate tribute to our departed friends and the friends of our ancestors, manifested in the security with which we guard their remains, and in the neatness with which we adorn the spot where they are deposited, is no less honorable to the survivors than it is respectful to the dead. "Our fathers," says an eloquent old writer, "find their graves in our short memories, and sadly tell us how we may be buried in our survivors." It is a good help to these " short memories," and a more than pardonable vanity, to keep recollection alive by monuments that may attract the eye and arrest the step, long after the bones beneath them shall have become part of the common mould.

I think we too much neglect this care of the dead. No one can travel through our land without being impressed with a disagreeable sense of our indifference to the adornment and even to the safety of the burial places. How often have I stopped to note the village grave-yard, occupying a cheerless spot by the road-side! Its ragged fence furnishing a scant and ineffectual barrier against the invasion of trespassing cattle, or beasts still more destructive; its area deformed with rank weeds,—the jamestown, the dock, and the mullen; and for shade, no better furniture than some dwarfish, scrubby, incongruous tree, meagre of leaves, gnarled and ungraceful, rising solitary above the coarse, unshorn grass. And there were the graves,—an unsightly array of naked mounds; some with no more durable memorial to tell who dwelt beneath, than a decayed, illegible tablet of wood, or if if better than this, the best of them with coverings of crumbling brick masonry and dislocated slabs of marble, forming perchance, family groups, environed by a neglected paling of dingy black, too plainly showing how entirely the occupancy had gone from the thoughts of their survivors. Not a pathway was there to indicate that here had ever come the mourner to look upon the grave of a friend, or that this was the haunt of a solitary footstep, bent hither for profitable meditation. I felt myself truly amongst the *deserted* mansions of the dead, and have turned from the spot to seek again the haunts of the living, out of the very chill of the heart which such a dilapidated scene had cast upon me. Many such places of interment may be found in the country.

It is scarce better in the cities. There is more expense, it is true and more care—for the tribute paid to mortality in the crowded city renders the habitations of its dead a more frequent resort. But in what concerns the garniture of these cemeteries, in all that relates to the embellishment appropriate to their character and their purpose, how much is wanting! Examine around our own city. You shall find more than one grave-yard enclosed with but the common post and rail fence and occupying the most barren spot of ground, in a suburb near to where the general offal of the town is strewed upon the plain and taints the air with its offensive exhalations. You will observe it studded with tombs of sufficiently neat structure, but unsoftened by the shade of a single shrub—or, if not entirely bare, still so naked of the simple ornament of tree and flower, as to afford no attraction to the eye, no solicitation to the footstep of the visitor. That old and touching appeal "*siste viator*," is made to the wayfarer from its desolate marbles in vain; there is nothing to stop the traveler and wring a sigh from his bosom, unless it be to find mortality so cheaply dealt with in these uncheery solitudes. We have cemeteries better than these, where great expense has been incurred to give them greater security and more elaborate ornament; but these too—even the best of them—are sadly repulsive to the feelings, from the air of overcrowed habitation, and too lavish expenditure of marble and granite within their narrow limits. This press for space, the result of an under-estimate, in the infancy of the city, of what time might require, has compelled the exclusion of that rural adornment so appropriate to the dwellings of the dead,—so appropriate because so pure and natural—the deep shade, the verdant turf, the flower-enamelled bank, with their concomitants, the hum of bees and carol of summer birds I like not these lanes of ponderous granite pyramids, these gloomy unwindowed blocks of black and white marble, these prison-shaped walls, and that harsh gate of rusty iron, slow moving on its grating hinges! I cannot affect this sterile and sunny solitude. Give me back the space the quiet, the simple beauty and natural repose of the country!

The profitable uses of the Cemetery are not confined to the security it affords the dead: The living may find in it a treasure of wholesome instruction. That heart which does not seek communion with the grave, and dwell with calm and even pleasurable meditation on the charge which nature's great ordinance has decreed, has laid up but scant provision against the weariness or the perils of this world's pilgrimage. "Measure not thyself by thy morning shadow, but by the extent of thy grave," is the solemn invocation which the departed spirit whispers into the ear of the living man. The tomb is a faithful counsellor, and may not wisely be estranged from our view. It tells us the great truth that Death is not the Destroyer, but Time; it counsels us that Time is our friend or foe, as we ourselves fashion him, and it warns us to make a friend of Time for the sake of Eternity. That this instruction may be often repeated and planted deep in our minds, I would have the public burial ground not remote from our habitations. It should be seated in some nook so peaceful and pleasant as to beguile the frequent rambler to its shades and win him to the contemplation of himself And though it should not be far from the dwellings of men, yet neither should it be cheapened in their eyes by bordering too obviously on the path of their common daily out-doings. Screens of thick foliage should shut it out from the road-side, or reveal it only in such glimpses as might show the wayfarer the sequesterment of the spot, and raise in his mind a respect for the reverence with which the slumber of the dead has been secured. There should evergreens relieve the bleak landscape of winter, and blooming thickets render joyous the approach of spring Amongst these should rise the monuments of the departed. Here, a lowly tablet, half hid beneath the plaited vines, to tell of some quiet, unobtrusive spirit that, even in the grave, had sought the modest privilege of being not too curiously scanned by the world; there, a rich column on the beetling brow of the hill, with its tasteful carvings and ambitious sculpture, to note the resting place of some favorite of fame or fortune. At many an interval, peering through the shubbery, the variously wrought tombs should unfold to the eye of the observer a visible index to that world of character which death had subdued into silence and group together under these diversified emblems of his power. There, matron and maid, parent and child, friend and brother, should be found so associated that their very environments should communicate something the story of their lives. Every thing around him should inspire the visitor with the sentiment that he walked among the relics of a generation dear to its survivors. The sanctity and silence of the place, with its quiet walks, its retired seats beneath overhanging boughs, its brief histories chronicled in stone, and its moral lessons uttered by speaking marble,—all these should allure him to meditate upon that great mystery of the grave, and teach him to weigh the vocations of this atom of time against the concerns of that long eternity upon which these tenants of the tomb had already entered. What heart-warnings would he gather in that meditation against the enticements of worldly favor! How soberly would he learn to reckon the chances of slippery ambition, the rewards of fortune, and the gratifications of sense!

We misjudge the world if we deem that even the most thoughtless of mankind have not a chord in their hearts to vibrate to the solemn harmony of such an atmosphere as this There is no slave of passion so dull to the persuasions of conscience, no worldling so bold in defying the proper instinct of his manhood, but would sometimes steal to a place like this to discourse with his own heart upon the awful question of futurity. Here would he set him down at the base of some comrade's recently erected tomb, and make a reckoning of his own fleeting day and then, with resolve of better life—a resolve which even the habit of his heedless career, perchance, has not power to stifle—go forth stoutly bent on its achievement Hither, in levity, would stray many a careless footstep, but not in levity depart. The chance caught warning of the tomb would attemper the mind to a sober tone of virtue, and long afterwards linger upon the memory. To this resort, the heart perplexed with wordly strivings and wearied with the appointments of daily care, would fly for the very relief of that lesson on the vanity of human pursuits which this mute scene would teach with an eloquence passing human endurance.

Such considerations as these have not been without their weight in prompting the enterprise which we are assembled this day to commemorate Our friends to whom the city is indebted for this design, have with great judgment and success, in the se'ection of the place and in the organization of their plan, sought to combine the benefit of these moral influences with the external or physical advantages of such an institution. The Cemetery, like those which suggested its establishment, will be maintained under regulations adapted to the preservation of every public observance of respect which the privacy and the sanctity of the purposes to which it is dedicated may require. Indeed, such institutions of themselves appeal so forcibly to the better instincts of our nature, and raise up so spontaneously sentiments of respect in the human bosom, as to stand in need of little rigor in the enforcement of the laws necessary to guard against violation. The experience of our people in their usefulness is limited to but few years; yet, brief as is the term, it is worthy of observation that no public establishment seems to have excited a more affectionate interest in the mind of the country, or enlisted a readier patronage than this mode of providing for the repose of the dead. Within the last ten years, the cemeteries of Mount Auburn and Laurel Hill have been constructed. They already constitute the most attractive objects to the research of the visitor in the environs of the cities to which they belong. Scarce an inhabitant of Boston or Philadelphia who does not testify to the pride with which he regards the public cemetery in his neighborhood. No traveler, with the necessary leisure on his hands, is content to quit those cities without an excursion to Mount Auburn or Laurel Hill; and the general praise of the public voice is expressed in every form in which the home dweller or the stranger can find utterance to pay a tribute to these beautiful improvements of the recent time.

This Cemetery of Greenmount constructed on the same plan, may advantageously compare with those to which I have alluded. It is more accessible than Mount Auburn; it is more spacious than that in the neighborhood of Philadelphia; and, in point of scenery, both as respects the improvement of the grounds, and the adjacent country, it is, at least equal to either. I know not where the eye may find more pleasant landscapes than those which surround us. Here, within our enclosures. how aptly do these sylvan embellishments harmonize with the design of the place!—this venerable grove of ancient forest; this lawn, shaded with choicest trees; that green meadow, where the brook creeps through the tangled thicket begemmed with wild flowers; these embowered alleys and pathways hidden in shrubbery, and that grassy knoll studded with evergreens and sloping to the cool dell where the fountain ripples over its pebbly bed:—all hemmed in by yon natural screen of foliage which seems to separate this beautiful spot from the world and devote it to the tranquil uses to which it is now to be applied. Beyond the gate that guards these precincts, we gaze upon a landscape rife with all the charms that hill and dale, forest-clad heights and cultured fields may contribute to enchant the eye. That stream which northward cleaves the woody hills, comes murmuring to our feet, rich with the reflections of the bright heaven and the green earth; thence leaping along between its granite banks, hastens towards the city whose varied outline of tower, steeple and dome, gilded by the evening sun and softened by the haze, seems to sleep in perspective against the southern sky: and there, fitly stationed within our view, that noble column, destined to immortality from the name it bears, lifts high above the ancient oaks that crown the hill, the venerable form of the Father of his Country a majestic image of the deathlessness of virtue.

Though scarce an half hour's walk from yon living mart where
one hundred thousand human beings toil in their noisy crafts, here
the deep quiet of the country reigns, broken by no ruder voice
than such as marks the tranquility of rural life.—the voice of "birds
on branches warbling,"—the lowing of distant cattle and the whet-
ting of the mower's scythe.   Yet tidings of the city not unpleasant-
ly reach the ear in the faint murmur, which at interval's, is borne
hither upon the freshening breeze, and more gratefully still in
the deep tones of that cathedral bell,

Swinging slow with sullen roar,

as morning and noon, and richer at eventide, it flings its pealing
melody across these shades with an invocation that might charm
the lingering visitor to prayer.

To such a spot as this have we come to make provision for our
long rest; and hither, even as drop follows drop in the rain, shall
the future generations that may people our city find their way,
and sleep at our sides.   It may be a vain fancy, yet still it is not
unpleasing, that in that long future our present fellowships may be
preserved, and that the friends and kindred who now cherish their
living association shall not be far separated in the tomb.   Here is
space for every denomination of religious society, leaving room for
each to preserve its appropriate ceremonies; and here too may
the city set apart a quarter for public use   That excellent custom,
the more excellent because it is so distinctly classical in its origin,
of voting a public tomb to eminent citizens, a custom yet unknown
to us, I trust, will, in the establishment of this Cemetery, find an
argument for its adoption : that here may be recorded the public
gratitude to a public benefactor; and in some conspicuous division
of these grounds, the stranger may read the history of the states-
man, the divine, the philanthropist, the soldier or the scholar,
whose deeds have improved, or whose fame adorned the city.   In
such monuments virtue finds a cheering friend, youth a noble in-
centive, and the heart of every man a grateful topic of remem-
brance.   I mistake our fellow-citizens if it would not gratify them
to see their public authorities adopt this custom.

There is something in the spectacle of a living generation
employed in the selection of their own tombs that speaks favorably
for their virtue   It testifies to a rational, reflecting piety; it tells
of life unhaunted by the terrors of death, of sober thought, and
serene reckoning of the past day.   Our present meditations have
not unreasonably fallen upon these topics, and I would fain hope
that they will leave us somewhat the wiser at our parting.   The
very presence of this scene, in connection with the purpose
that brought us hither, sheds a silent instruction on the heart.
How does it recall the warning of Scripture, "Go to now, ye that
say to-day or to morrow we will go into such a city, and continue
there a year, and buy and sell and get gain ; whereas ye know not
what shall be on the morrow.   For what is your life ? It is even

a vapor that appeareth for a little time and then vanisheth away."
This grove now untenanted by a single lodger, this upland plain,
and all these varied grounds, in the brief space of a few generations, shall become a populous dwelling-place of the dead. Hither
then will come the inmates of you rapidly-increasing city, in their
holiday walks, to visit our tombs, and gaze upon the thick-strewed
monuments that shall meet them on every path Amongst these
some calm moralist of life, some thoughtful observer of man and
his aims, will apply himself 'here to study the past—his past,
and whilst he lingers over the inscriptions that shall tell him
of this busy crowd, who intently ply what we deem the important
labors of to-day,—alas, how shrunk and dwarfed shall we appear
in his passing comment! A line traced by the chisel upon
the stone shall tell all, and more perhaps than posterity may be
concerned to know, about us and our doings. Which of us shall
reach a second generation in that downward journey of fame?
How many of these events which now fill our minds, as matters
belonging to the nation's destiny, shall stand recorded before the
eye of that aftertime? How much of our personal connection with
present history, these strivings of ours to be noted in the descent
of time, these clamorous invocations of posterity, these exaggera-
tions of ourselves and our deeds shall be borne even to the begin-
ning of the next half-century? Here is a theme for human vanity!
Let it teach us humility, and in humility that wisdom which shall
set us to so ordering our lives, that in our deaths those who
survive us may be instructed how to win the victory over
the grave. Then shall our monuments be more worthy to be
cherished by future generations, and the common doom of
oblivion, perchance, be averted by better remembrances than
these legends on our tombs. In this anticipation we may find
something not ungrateful in the thoughts, that whilst all mortal
beings march steadily onward " to cold obstruction," we sink into
our gradual dust upon a couch chosen by ourselves, with many
memorials of friendship and esteem clustered around our remains,
and that there we shall sleep secure until the last summons shall
command the dead to arise, and call us into the presence of a mer-
ciful God.

It does not fall to my province to pursue these reflections within
the confines to which they so plainly lead us. Such topics belong
to a more solemn forum, and a better provided orator; I dare not
invade their sacred field. My task required no more than that I
should present those public considerations which have induced the
establishment of this Cemetery; the subject has naturally brought
me to the verge of that sublime mystery, from which, in reverence
only, I turn back my steps.

In closing my duties at this point, I may assume, without tran-
scending my assigned privilege, to speak a parting word. Our
thoughts have been upon the grave—our discourse has been
of death. It is good for us to grow familiar with this theme; but
only good, as weighing its manifold conditions, we deduce from
the study of its urgent persuasions to a life of piety and virtue.

"So live that when thy summons comes to join
The innumerable caravan that moves
To the pale realms of shade, where each shall take
His chamber in the silent halls of Death,
Thou go not like the quarry slave at night,
Scourg'd to his dungeon : but sustain'd and sooth'd
By an unfaltering trust approach thy grave
Like one who wraps the drapery of his couch
About him, and lies down to pleasant dreams."

HYMN.

BY FRANK H. DAVIDGE, ESQ.

FOUNT of mercies—source of love,
   List the hymns we raise to thee ;
From thy holy throne above,
   Heedful of our worship be.

Creatures of thy sov'reign will,
   At thy feet we humbly bend ;
Let thy grace our bosoms fill,
   Be our comfort—be our friend.

Here beneath the sunlit sky,
   With thy gifts around us spread ;
We beseech thee—from on high—
   Bless these dwellings of the dead.

Guard them when the summer's glow,
   Decks with beauties, hill and dale ;
Guard them when the winter's snow,
   Spreads o'er all its mantle pale.

Here—when wearied pilgrims cease,
   O'er life's chequered scenes to roam,
May their ashes rest in peace,
   'Till thy voice shall call them home.

Then, oh then—their trials done,
   Bid them rise to worship thee,
Where the ransomed of thy Son,
   Join in endless harmony.

The ceremonies of the dedication were then concluded with a Benediction from the REV. J. G. HAMNER, Pastor of the Fifth Presbyterian Church in Baltimore.

THE FIRST GRAVE.

BY S. T. WALLIS, ESQ.

The city of the dead hath thrown wide its gates at last,
And, through the cold gray portal, a fun'ral train hath passed—
One grave—the first—is open, and on its lonely bed,
Some heir of sin and sorrow hath come to lay his head.

Perchance a hero cometh, whose chaplet, in its bloom,
Hath fallen from his helmet, to wither on his tomb :
It may be that hot youth comes—it may be we behold,
Here, broken at the cistern, pale beauty's bowl of gold.

Mayhap that manhood's struggle, despite of pride and power,
Hath ended in the darkness and sadness of this hour,
Perchance some white-haired pilgrim, with travel sore oppressed.
Hath let his broken staff fall, and bent him down to rest.

But stay, behold the sepulchre! nor age, nor strength is there ;
Nor fame, nor pride, nor manhood, those lagging mourners bear;
A little child is with them,* as pale and pure as snow,
Her mother's tears not dry yet, upon her gentle brow !

The step that tottered, trembling,—the heart that faltered too,
At the faintest sound of terror the infant spirit knew—
The eyes that glistened, tearful, when shadowy eve came on—
Now show no dread of sleeping in darkness and alone.

And why, though all be lonely, should that young spirit fear,
Through midnight and through tempest—no shielding bosom near?
Ere the clod was on the coffin—ere the spade had cleft the clod—
Bright angels clad a fellow in the raiment of their God !

Green home of future thousands! how blest in sight of heaven,
Are these, the tender firstlings, that death to thee has given !
Though prayer and solemn anthem have echoed from thy hill,
This first, fresh grave of childhood, hath made thee holier still !

The morning flowers that deck thee, shall sweeter, lovelier, bloom
Above the spot where beauty, like theirs, hath found a tomb,
And when the evening cometh, the very stars shall keep
A vigil, as of seraphs, where innocence doth sleep !

Sweet hope! that, when the slumbers of thy pilgrims shall be o'er
And the valley of death's shadow hath mystery no more,
To them, the trumpet's clangor may whisper accents mil'd,
And bid them wear the garlands that crown this little child.

1845.

*The first person buried in Greenmount Cemetery was an infant.

Human Sepulture.

FROM the remotest antiquity human sepulture has received special attention from the nations of the earth.

The remotest traditions and records of people indicate that inhumation or earth-burial was the kind most generally practiced.

The first recorded instance of human burial is found in Genesis, "And Abraham buried Sarah, his wife, in the cave of the field of Machpelat."

Jacob, when he was about to die, charged his sons to bury him in the cave with his fathers,—for the reason that "There they buried Abraham and Sarah his wife,—there they buried Isaac and Rebecca, his wife,—and there he had buried Leah." And when Jacob died, his sons carried him into the land of Canaan and buried him in the cave in the field of Machpelat.

When, after the crucifixion, Pilate gave the body of Christ to Joseph, he took it down from the cross—wrapped it in linen and laid it in a sepulchre hewn in the rock, and rolled a stone before the mouth. Only three witnesses and mourners were present at this burial of Jesus,—Joseph, Mary Magdalene and Mary the mother of James, of Joses, and Salome.

Some oriental nations resorted to burning the dead body—cremation, and preserved the ashes in urns—urn burial—or placed them in coffins rapidly destructive to the flesh—sarcophagi—flesh-eating.

The ancient Egyptians and others practiced embalming, and the embalmed bodies of their kings were deposited in chambers and niches of their Pyramids.

The ancient mounds and tumuli found throughout the western area of this Continent, 10,000 of them being in the State of Ohio alone, and in Mexico and Peru, were the mausolea of the distinguished dead of these ancient and extinct races who erected them.

The North American Indians in the burial of their dead practiced a rude mode of embalming, and in the place of inhumation or earth-burial, deposited them upon a rude platform elevated above the ground.

The Greeks and Romans were renowned for the refinement and taste they displayed in the adornment of their burial places, and the genius of the sculptor was never more happily evoked than when employed to preserve in imperishable marble some royal personage, glorious hero or radiant beauty.

Grecian classic literature describes the ancient mode of burial, and Homer in Hellenic verse describes the pomp and magnificence of Athenian burial.

Most of the nations of antiquity buried their dead outside their city walls, from a dread apprehension of a pestilential influence of dead bodies; and the ancient Romans were forbidden by a law of the twelve tables to bury within the walls of ancient Rome.

Upon nearly all Roman grave-stones was inserted "*Liste Viator—*"

"HALT TRAVELLER."

Henry W. Jenkins.   Thos. W. Jenkins.

HENRY W. JENKINS & SON,

No. 16 Light Street.

Furnishing Undertakers

Residence of Henry W. Jenkins,

164 BARRE STREET.

Residence of Thomas W. Jenkins,

70 SARATOGA STREET.

www.ingramcontent.com/pod-product-compliance
Lightning Source LLC
Chambersburg PA
CBHW030911260626
47169CB00008B/2797